Musings on the Ethics of Growth

AuthorHouse™ UK
1663 Liberty Drive
Bloomington, IN 47403 USA
www.authorhouse.co.uk
Phone: 0800.197.4150

© 2015 Hamthesketch. All rights reserved.

No part of this book may be reproduced, stored in a retrieval system, or transmitted by any means without the written permission of the author.

Published by AuthorHouse 07/14/2015

ISBN: 978-1-5049-4279-9 (sc)
ISBN: 978-1-5049-4284-3 (e)

Print information available on the last page.

Any people depicted in stock imagery provided by Thinkstock are models, and such images are being used for illustrative purposes only. Certain stock imagery © Thinkstock.

This book is printed on acid-free paper.

Because of the dynamic nature of the Internet, any web addresses or links contained in this book may have changed since publication and may no longer be valid. The views expressed in this work are solely those of the author and do not necessarily reflect the views of the publisher, and the publisher hereby disclaims any responsibility for them.

Musings on the Ethics of Growth

Hamthesketch

authorHOUSE

Hamish Simpson
Architect Illustrator

140, Thornhill Road, Streetly, *Diparch.*
Sutton Coldfield, *ARIBA.*
West Midlands. B74 2ED. UK. *FSAI.*
  retired

phone : 0121 353 4766.
email : hamish.simpson051@btinternet.com
web : www.hamthesketch.co.uk

A prickly read containing food for thought.

The Author... Hamthesketch

Born in Largs, Scotland at the outbreak of world war two, the author has always been curious about the chancy nature of life. Over 70 years of rapid social changes, his architect experience, worldwide travel and his observation of flora and fauna have developed an awareness of the fragile nature of the planet and of our vulnerability to excessive, rapid growth.

The war resulted in the loss of his father and uprooting his family to Sutton Coldfield, England. His concerns inspired him to write about aspirations, and why they are so difficult to achieve. He is convinced that natural desires to grow and prosper have to be compatible with earth's limited capacity. He has come to believe the power of science to enhance innovation, growth and prosperity has blinded us all to our ultimate reliance on the good health of our planet.

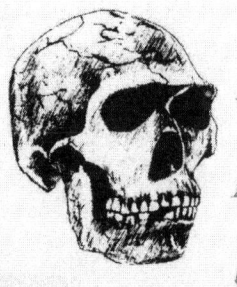

40,000 years from Neanderthal to Civilised man.

Civilised man to Scatterbrain, 100 years.

Scatterbrain to Bananas, any time now.

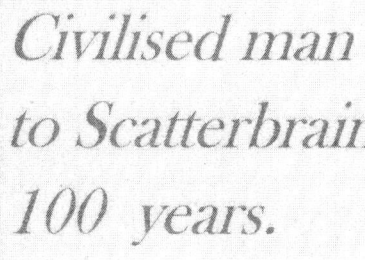

Population and Consumption are driving us INSANE

Musings on the Ethics of Growth

Introduction

In trying to think how to improve our daily lives a common theme was revealed. Whichever subject was chosen, peeling back the layers of surface trivia always exposed a core of optimism for growth.

Historic enthusiasm for progress had always been possible because there used to be space and time to achieve our aspirations.

Present growth policies are still based on processes which created the Industrial Revolution, when population was about 1.5 billion. They are no longer able to cope with ordinary humanitarian needs of the expanding 7 billion.

Political, economic, commercial and social processes are reaching the limits of sustainability.

The challenge for the 21st century is to reduce growth to compatible proportions, with the earth's finite capacity and with our insatiable demands.

I hope this booklet will encourage thought and discussion, beyond daily frustrations, to consideration of our present global predicament.

Articles	Contents	Pages
1.	Ethical Growth	8
2.	Basic Concerns	9
3.	Purpose of Religion	10,11
4.	Advantage of Marriage	12,13
5.	Hetero - Homo Hiatus	14,15
6.	Conundrum of Growth	16
7.	Edifying Education	17
8.	NHS in need of Care	18,19
9.	Local Autonomy	20,21
10.	Desperate Developments	22,23
11.	Immigrant Impasse	24,25
12.	Social Ineptitude	26,27
13.	Social Justice	28,29
14.	Cry for Democracy	30,31
15.	Europe, your Options	32,33
16.	Climate-change Claptrap	34,35
17.	Energetic waste of Energy	36,37
18.	Wages of Sin	38,39
19.	Population, problem or Paranoia	40,41
20.	Art or Artful	42,43
21.	Reach for the Stars or Starve	44,45
22.	Our Civil Scenarios	46,47

Ethical Growth

One glorious dawn in Sutton Park, 60 years ago, the first sound of human activity came from distant chinking of bottles on an early milk round. That peace, only 8 miles from the centre of Birmingham, is now swamped by day and night rumble of noise.

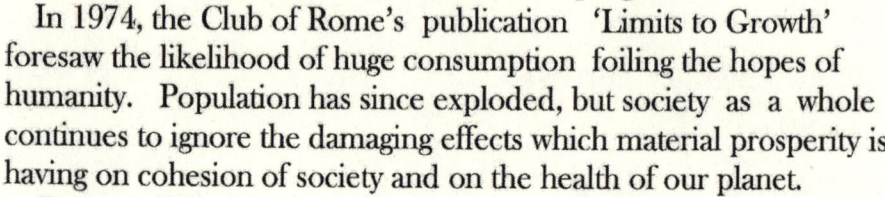

Noise is just a symptom of energy use, needed to provide requirements and whims of ever-increasing population. Success in finding new fuel sources has encouraged yet more growth, but to what end ? Frenetic despoliation of our planet is not what I call progress.

In 1974, the Club of Rome's publication 'Limits to Growth' foresaw the likelihood of huge consumption foiling the hopes of humanity. Population has since exploded, but society as a whole continues to ignore the damaging effects which material prosperity is having on cohesion of society and on the health of our planet.

Communities used to evolve around local industry. They had identity and human scale. We are now in a permanent 'catch-up' economy, run by centralised mass-production, creating uniformity and impersonal services. Rate of change prevents everyone from looking where we are going. Short-term solutions are creating environments foreign to our well-being. At some stage population will be curtailed. If not by our conscious efforts, the implacable constraints of the planet will do the job for us.

Basic Concerns

In the 60's I was aware my leafy neighbourhood was being overrun by building developments. Post-war enthusiasm for tearing away the old to provide new facilities caused a vague worry and sense of loss. The spread of housing and industry has now covered all my childhood haunts with urbanisation.

The process used to be slow. Expansion is now so rapid that there is no time to adjust. Our surroundings have become bland and our services complex, while the cost of living has soared.

Current innovative processes create ever more technical solutions, controlled by ever larger and more powerful conglomerates who's aims are profit, not enhancement of daily life. Glossy advertising encourages everyone to keep up with the Jones's. We have become a subservient component in an industrial machine which is despoiling the earth for the sake of short term material gain. The process is eliminating our natural inheritance on which everything ultimately depends.

Use of unrenewable recourses, profligacy and corruption blight potential advantages that techno-

science could provide. Beyond the sparkling cities and wizardry of the electronic age, evidence of severe global deterioration should cause us to take notice of what is happening.

Malthus, Orwell and Huxley deserve better than ridicule. Their scenarios become ever closer to reality as we become more controlled by technology and oppressive authority.

Purpose of Religion

Since the beginning of time, evolving life has depended on the forces and physical components of our universe. Species have evolved by the impersonal process of trial and error as environmental conditions changed. Only the lucky few survived to face yet more change as the earth slowly aged. Emergence of the human race left behind a tree of spreading branches which failed to adapt.

Our consciousness is unique. It possesses intelligence, enabling self-determination and imagination. Man has always been aware of something greater than himself. There had to be a reason for existence, and a source of comfort to ameliorate the harsh realities of pain and death. That he depended on nature was first acknowledged through ceremony, showing respect for his fellow creatures and for the land on which he lived. There was an innate desire to express his wonder and thanks for life, and to reveal his fear of and subservience to his maker.

This reverence was later symbolised by devotion to symbolic Gods which precipitated a hierarchy of religious leaders. Our thanks and devotion were transformed to adoration of artificial replicas. But enlightenment came from ancient teachers who preached a benign moral code, applicable to every individual. It encouraged restraint, consideration of others and the need to be conscious and caring of the natural world.

As population and civilisations grew, it developed into specific religions, having different cultural expression. These differences have multiplied and deviated, many into self-serving organisations where symbolism, idolatry and closed minds have conspired to serve the hierarchy, not the people and their source of well-being.

The possibility of continued healthy evolution depends on obedience to the fundamental laws of nature, not on spectacular material advances and rape of the earth, which even now are despoiling the planet and leaving half the population in deprivation.

What has come to be known as religion is so disguised by diversity and the trappings of ceremony, that it's original benign disciplines are lost. The name of, and devotion to one's particular creed is secondary to the essence of the original message. There was, and still is, good reason to adhere to those original teachings.

Freedoms without the disciplines of responsibility have created frenetic chaos which now dominates and endangers all life. Legitimate desires for good health and prosperity will not be achieved through narrow self-interest, indiscriminate use of technology and perpetual growth. Earth's capacity is physically restricted, and humanity will have to come to understand that expansion of civilisation also has it's limits. Personal desires amount to wishful thinking when put in context with implacable forces which created us. Experience and knowledge illustrate that we remain the subjects of chance, not the rulers of life.

Morality is a basic requirement of humanity. It's purpose is still based on providing the best chance of tolerable survival on our world which is subject to powers beyond our ken and control.

Advantage of Marriage

'Vive la difference'

Love, sex and marriage are possible in any combination. We do not know how our ancestors divided their preferences, but some must have chosen sex between male and female, with or without love or marriage. Child birth has depended on hetero-sexual procreation.

The exclusive nature of the coupling began to be acknowledged through public ceremony, and later religious vows ensured the intent of long term commitment for protection of the offspring, as well as for security of both partners. Peer pressure encouraged the couple to stick together. The extended family was always there to provide support in good and bad times. The community at large was consequently saved from having to look after other people's children.

Human nature, being so fickle, and primitive instincts so strong, commitment was a big ask. As prosperity spread, search for work caused families to split apart. Without strong community influences, the new economic freedoms permitted infidelity and damaging sexual behaviours to proceed unhindered. Broken marriages, premature sex and children being born outside of wedlock became a social nightmare.

So the growing need for care and support of disadvantaged women and children was taken over by the state. Through the state's authority we are now obliged to pay for other's unconventional behaviour via national taxation.

Apart from the insult to those who are not directly responsible, this has resulted in eliminating any need to adhere to the nation's moral codes. Those codes of behaviour had evolved over millennia to provide stability in social affairs,... a basic requirement for productive development of civilised life. Distancing birth and nurturing from the biological parents endangers the well-being of child, parent. and society.

State intervention may have prevented extreme deprivation, but it is now overwhelmed by the size, complexity and cost of demand.

The rest of us are now obliged to contribute to broken families, co-habiting, single parents and misplaced children. Lack of personal responsibility, deprivation and assumption that the state will provide have created an unstable base for modern society. Traditional marriage has been the foundation of society. Family life, which requires commitment, tolerance and self-sacrifice has never been easy. To transfer responsibility from the wayward to those who all ready bear the burden of national social cohesion may be well-intended, but it belittles the importance of marriage and is overwhelming the state's ability to cope.

We are not ready for Brave New World. Refusal to accept benign disciplines is placing us in jeopardy of living emasculated lives where existence is reduced to gratification of immediate desires and obedience to oppressive authority. That authority would be better employed in upholding the virtues of personal responsibility, restraint and long term commitment.

Present instability of social systems is largely a consequence of hasty decline of marriage in favour of apparent modern freedoms. Family and state require stability which traditional marriage would help to recreate.

Hetero - Homo Hiatus
'Vive les differences'

If you have ever cut a finger or suffered other bodily damage, it soon becomes apparent that each element of the body has evolved to have a purpose. Without use, even of a small part, one is in-convenience, or worse. When one element does not work, other parts, including the sub-conscious brain, attempt to compensate. Considering the sex drive, it is astonishing that it can be replicated by other means.

Hetero and Homo sexuality are innately potential. One of the combinations can result in child birth, the others can not. The difference is fundamental to human relationships.

Reproduction has always been the prime function of all living matter, including us. Our survival depends on hetero-sexual procreation. For centuries it was so successful that communities revered it and developed ceremonies to sustain it. This 'normal' arrangement was so entrenched that it became the automatic foundation of society, and alternative coupling arrangements became outlawed. Homo-sexuality was widely regarded as deviant.

There is doubt why variations in sexual behaviour have been so persistent, and much confusion about their status. However, as prosperity and new freedoms developed there appeared to be room for tolerance and acceptance of alternative life styles. Homo-sexuality is now officially OK, although it will take decades for the concept to be accepted by everyone.

Desire of some homo-sexual partners to be married is understandable. They share the same need for comfort and security as the rest of us. But insistence for religious vows and acquisition of children is illogical, socially dangerous and emotionally doubtful. It is difficult to accept that their chosen life-styles, which exclude the possibility of natural child birth, should then be equipped with the trappings of religious vows and children. Biological and emotional requirements are absent, and traditional marriage is undermined.

At the same time, a consequence of normal relationships being so successful has resulted in a population explosion. There is presently a growing in-balance between social appetite and the means of feeding it. Recent acceptance of homo-sexuality is not only a pragmatic solution to a human rights issue, it may be a totally subconscious attempt to balance the equation of too many people in too small a place.

The ideal need for children to be produced and nurtured by their own biological parents, for the physical and mental health of everyone concerned, only works when there is affordable space, water, food and shelter. These provisions are know to be deteriorating as population increases.

It may be wise to welcome homo-sexuality and void relationships as they help to reduce the principal cause of present worldwide stress. But the differences between hetero and homo have to be recognised and maintained.

Conundrum of Growth

Does one ignore, pick up and pocket, or donate to charity, that £10 note lying in the gutter? Is it sensible to satisfy an immediate need while ignoring future outcome? Legitimate attempts to improve one's lot tend to exclude unintended consequences in the wider context.

Like water under gravity, we are in fact compelled to take the least line of resistance. It may not seem so when one's personal wishes are set aside to assist someone else, but the 'feel good' or 'guilt factors' are sufficient to determine the least line of resistance. If the £note is given to charity, altruism wins the day. If £it is pocketed, genuine need or pure greed have taken precedence. To ignore £it altogether implies there are other things on one's mind.

Society is full of such anomalies. The greatest for me is why our dependence on the momentum of growth takes precedence over consequent depletion of our means of existence. Mathematically it is not possible to squeeze a gallon into a pint pot. The attempt is messy and 7 pints are wasted. The pint pot is just not big enough.

Last century, when there was room for the horse-driven economy to be overtaken by the motor, rail and aircraft industries, the point was less obvious. Nowadays, as compounding rate of change overwhelms the land, there are fewer options for expansion.

Overcrowding, scarcities, deprivation and disease are negating hopes of prosperity for all. Even the powerful are at risk of decline.

Quelle dommage

Edifying Education

Attainment of examination success is a very poor guide to the usefulness of education. The curricula has been biased to the arts and has neglected the value of practical skills.

Academia has not learned how to relate it's knowledge and experience to modern life. Graduating students have little appreciation of how to use their limited knowledge in our rapidly changing environment.

Ivory Tower aspirations have not enjoyed the benefits of small classes, calm discipline and time to think. They have no appreciation of our total inter-dependence. Pursuit of affluence has created an elite who regard dirty hands with disdain, yet they depend on the products of those hands. Basic principals and the paramount requirement to think require reinstatement.

Of course academia is important, but a professor who sits on a Chippendale chair tends to be uncaring of the extraordinary skill and poor wages of the craftsman who made it. Mediocrity of our expanding built environment indicates complacency of the need for physical care of our services and surroundings. Dumbing-down of quality and standards, and prevailing carelessness are products of the present system. Picking up your litter is just as important as picking up your certificate of education.

Education has to embrace individual responsibility for social and environmental conditions. Subjects in the curricula have to relate to the challenges of excessive consumption, pure waste, and overcrowding if they are to have any relevance to the 21st century.

NHS in need of Care

The post-war concept of a national health service, free at the point of entry, was based on clinical need rather than on ability to pay. It was divided into 3 basic functions, Hospital services, Primary care and Community services. The tax payer paid the bills, it was a bed of roses.

Size and complexity of the organisation are now so huge, it is demonstrably too large to administer efficiently. The rate at which new cures become available and the demographic in-balance of population cause anomalies in the service and patient dissatisfaction.

It is not the fault of the NHS that we become ill or suffer accident. That is the patients' misfortune, and in any circumstance, we should be grateful that it has been so successful and lasted so long. But the complexity of administering real-estate and services to satisfy ever-increasing demand is no longer sustainable. Tax payers are becoming fewer as the aged increase.

The situation is complicated by private health care which depends on payment at the point of entry. Logic and rational have to come

into play. There is a desperate need to revert to basic principals, to distinguish which ailments are appropriate for free treatment and which are irrelevant, or more appropriate to private care.

If it is to remain a beacon of civilised society, the NHS will have to limit it's responsibilities to what can realistically be managed, and to locate t's services accordingly.

It is inevitable that analysis of the relative importance of any individual ailment or service would cause an outcry of horror. But to ignore the need to separate vital from less valid services will result in choking deterioration.

Practical and financial constraints may compromise location of services in the short term, but consideration of which ailments may be treated freely is less clear.

I'm afraid they must all be rearranged

As exercise and moderation are innate requirements for good health, should the wantonly careless be obliged to contribute ? Repair of one's face after being sprayed with acid should be free, but surgical manipulation for vanity's sake should not. The whole gambit of who and what is appropriate for free care has to be reconsidered, as it is all ready impossible to satisfy every need.

It is too easy to abuse the system with minor ailments and inappropriate tasks. At the other end of the scale, long life has increased need for replacement surgery, billions of pills and mental treatment. They can not all be afforded.

Even the doctors' ethical code has become outdated in the context of overcrowding and diminishing recourses. Every vestige of life is squeezed from half formed foetuses and the dying in the questionable 'name of humanity'. Technology and religious dogma determine when contraception and abortion are permitted. Little thought is given to overstressed services nor to the depraved condition of half the world's population.

Common sense itself has to be recovered.

Local Autonomy

Throughout the Commonwealth, British Independent Territories, and the UK itself, there is confusion over the status quo. Should the Channel Islands be French, should Gibraltar be Spanish, should the Falklands belong to Argentina and should the Commonwealth be disbanded?

Geography suggests they should, but historic, cultural, security and economic ties suggest they should not. Then there is Ireland. How odd it is for that small and beautiful island to be split in two and for the south to be separated. In Scotland's case it is superficially obvious that they remain part of the UK. But consistent reluctance of London-centric authority to acknowledge their legitimate concerns has caused a desire for independence. They are not alone. In post-war times, throughout the more rural areas of Britain, opportunities for productive work and share of national prosperity have been neglected. Discontent is widespread and growing.

Since decline of Clyde shipbuilding, loss of traditional jobs throughout the land has caused poverty and consequent migration to where alternative work was available. From London to Liverpool there is now such an increase in activity that their bursting conurbations are becoming unmanageable. They have concerns, but they relate to overcrowding.

In the UK, this in-balance is a principal cause of growing desire for local autonomy. In the context of Europe, individual nations are also becoming resentful of centralised, undemocratic power.

As authority becomes remote from personal and local interests people become resentful and disillusioned. Scotland's desire for independence reflects a common discontent throughout this nation and the whole of Europe about 'the way the world is going'. We are not just numbers on a chart, to be manipulated by global corporations, nor by their political slaves.

Concentration of power and wealth in London has to be shared more equably throughout the whole land for stability and lasting progress. Independence for Scotland would cause ignominy and weakness for each of the individual territories. It would encourage Wales and Northern Ireland to follow suit, leaving England's global influence in disarray, from which we would all suffer.

Prosperity is far more likely within a united kingdom, (including repatriation of Eire), if only London's power was shared. The constituent parts would be far more co-operative if they had a meaningful say in matters of national importance. Local districts would likewise be more content with some meaningful control over their varied local concerns.

Lasting prosperity will not happen without united co-operation. The present confrontational system is reduced to bickering over short term trivial matters, while matters of national strategy are dictated by isolated authority. The system is no longer fit for purpose. Local authority boundaries and land ownership presently restrict best use of our land and local recourses. A skeleton plan for the whole territory is required, based on the physical constraints, as well as on opportunities which our varied environment contains.

Desperate Developments

As the local rail station, post office, school and then the pub disappeared from rural communities, overcrowded conurbations and London-centric activity have combined to unbalance this land.

While the countryside is becoming a Disney folly, centres of population are becoming unmanageable. Real and present need for regeneration does not depend on massive indiscriminate building. Repeated experience has shown that every time mega extensions are built to improve capacity, they are quickly refilled to capacity by further growth. As with some large banks, London itself is thought to be too large to fail. So they invest in cross-rail and more complex mega-building, while it's inhabitants become inhibited by frenetic activity, restricted liberties and extreme costs. Is that the way the rest of us want to live?

Are our villages to morph into towns and our towns into cities and our cities into conglomerates un-suitable for healthy living ?

Rapid, crude expansion is destroying our heritage. It is being replaced by insensitive mono-culture, which itself will require regeneration within a few decades. For how long does establishment think the process can continue ?

Ultra high speed rail and motorway expansions may facilitate growth and mobility for a time. They also spread urban sprawl and congestion at enormous expense, but rural Britain will remain neglected. Global expansion to air traffic and container shipping may supply our appetites for a while. They also spread pollution, and risk total dependence on huge, remote and fallible organisations.

Profitable grandiose schemes do not provide what this country needs. That is,... Sustained security and stability, so that normal man can have some confidence that his home will retain it's value and services,... That work, schooling and health facilities are locally available,... That his castle will not be overwhelmed by encroachment of bland urbanisation.

The borrowed £billions would be better spent on re-invigorating unglamorous, but vital countrywide infrastructure, in all our essential services. Planning could retain what is worthy and control the scale of development appropriately to local circumstances. Local identity, local vernacular and local green spaces are important.

It comes back to population and outdated methods of valuing our priorities. To add 500 houses in a year, to a village which has taken 1000 years to evolve is neither pleasant or civilised.
Increasing the complexity of cities only keeps them functional in the short term.
Demands for continual growth create the anomalies and it is here that thought, open discussion and action is most needed. It is time to acknowledge that population is excessive and that controls have become necessary.

*And will those feet
in future time,
Walk on Britain's pastures green ?
And was the wise intent of God
In Britain's conurbations seen ?*

Immigrant Impasse

Without territorial boundaries, safety and sustenance for evolution would not have been possible. Marking of territory has been essential, whether by scenting the boundaries, or by surrounding them with barbed wire. In modern times the customs post ensures safe comings and goings between nations. In such sophisticated countries as ours', rape and pillage were no longer a threat.

More recent relaxation of control at the borders was thought to be a civilised solution to the growing mobility of populations. The only alternative reason is state incompetence, which could never be admitted. We now all know that consequent rapid increase to UK population is a direct result of excessive immigration.

The rate of increase and the total number of people now here has caused the greatest social upheaval in Britain's history. Ability to absorb the influx has less to do with colour or race, but more to do with the physical, emotional and organisational capacity of the host nation to cope. The influx is not temporary, and once here, many wish to retain their cultural identity and to settle where their kin are already established. But, from wherever they come, they are in a foreign land and must be required to adhere to the common language, culture and laws of their host. Our extraordinary tolerance in accommodating cultural differences, has to be alert to abuse of the rules.

More recent immigration has increased formation of ghettoes, obtrusive religious practices and cruel anti-social behaviour, as well as overstressing local services to the point of collapse. Any new religious group which becomes too large can not avoid having unwelcome influence over established communities. Stability and integration will not be achieved by appeasement to these extremes. Laws of the land, which have been hard-won for the benefit of the people as a whole, must be upheld, not just for protection from terrorism, but for the ordinary well being of civilised British life. That requires planning to prevent minority groups taking over local neighbourhoods and application of policies to control overall population.

European influences and government policies have enforced immigration, some of which is beneficial, but much of which supplies a bank of cheap labour, while the redundant survive on benefits, wallowing in despondent frustration.

We do not have the space which France and Germany enjoy. Mediocrity, disparity and substitution of integrity by carelessness, greed and dishonesty make plebs of us all, while our 'green and pleasant land' is becoming unrecognisable.

The miss-match of total population with available recourses derives from blinkered, short-term incompetence. It requires strategic planning to re-establish priorities. If that is beyond the wit of man, what use is our experience and education ?

Social Ineptitude

The stated intention of most democracies is to provide security and good health, so that economic and material prosperity may be achieved. But new freedoms which prosperity have given have lost sight of the meaning of progress. In our overcrowded lives it is rare to find contentment, let alone happiness. Fundamental need to feel safe and to enjoy the benefits which innovation has produced are being negated by speed of change and inane despoliation of what we know and love.

Moral integrity which used to encourage community spirit has been replaced by single-minded pursuit of material wealth, to the exclusion of the finer emotional requirements of humanity. Experiments with rats indicate that social cohesion brakes down as overcrowding and scarcities impinge. We no longer need such experiments as daily life proves the point.

On the foundation of the industrial revolution, population has increased so much, and so rapidly that pressures on land and recourses have become critical. Disproportionate exploitation of the powerful has left the rest in subservient poverty, and no one knows what to do for the best.

The profit motif has lead industry and politics up an endless spiral of wishful thinking, as they drag the populous behind in a trail of blind ignorance. Politicians offer empty promises in the vain hope of re-election to office. The public, grasping at straws, are falling into the black hole.

We remain complacent, until a particular problem lands on our door step. Only then do we wake-up, and then it is only to complain about someone else's incompetence.

No one is looking at the causes of so much global angst. Short term outlook is no longer adequate to overcome the consequences of excessive consumption and destruction of the environment Manipulation around the edge of growth policies is futile. It is the policies themselves which require radical change.

Favourable comparisons of our present enthusiasm for growth, with past successes are no longer valid. The appetite of present growth is so great that our reserves can not be replenished, no matter how clever the innovations. The intention to continue building our way out of the problem on borrowed £billions has created debt which can not be repaid by present generations. Is there no guilt, no concern for our children ?

Appeasement to popular demands can only disguise the true nature of our underlying problems. Surely there is all ready sufficient evidence of social and physical deterioration to start addressing those real underlying issues.

Science may keep the plates spinning for a while longer, but space and time are fast running out. Acknowledgement that population will have to be curtailed, and eventually reduced, is long overdue.

Co-operation in talking about solutions is a priority for everyone. We have the facilities. It would be tragic not to use them.

Social Justice

What is right or wrong, ultimately has to relate to what is good for human survival. Considering the overcrowded state of the planet, the Law has not yet come to terms with the damaging behaviour which humanity is inflicting on the health of society and on the planet itself.

Indiscriminate use of technology, uncontrolled use of unrenewable recourses, corruption and destruction of habitat are having far more serious consequences than any local crimes.

Justice has to recognise crimes against the planet, just as it does with crimes against humanity, as they are coming to mean the same thing. Advances in science and relaxation of traditional moral codes have provided personal freedoms which are destroying any concept of stable society. The power of large scale commerce has become a blight on sustainable progress. Prosperity for the lucky is causing poverty for most, and it is actively ruining the chances of tolerable living conditions for future generations.

Without acknowledgment of this predicament, the personal, local concerns of daily life can not be usefully addressed. Intricate rules to control daily activities in overcrowded situations will inevitably cause a plethora of misdemeanours. An undisciplined society is bound to provide opportunity for unsocial and criminal behaviour. When excessive disparity exists, it is inevitable that resentment will thrive and sense of community will dissipate.

Present law enforcement is erratic. It is the easy targets which receive predominant attention, yet they tend to be of nuisance value. Many who cause the greatest damage are so connected to establishment that they remain largely untouchable. The public requires a much clearer definition of what constitutes modern crime, and the Law has to break through the barrier of intimidation by those who possess the wealth and power.

In this country the death penalty is considered inappropriate, as conviction mistakes do happen. Physical punishment is considered inhumane. But is confining a person to jail for prolonged periods any more civilised ? Pain is the element which has discouraged damaging behaviour in all species since life began. Not to use it can seem like duty neglected, rather than a concession to civilised life.

There is ambiguity here. The intention of the law is surely to protect the public from crime in the most humane and affordable manner. Castration of paedophiles would provide an efficient service, but our squeamish reluctance to accept physical solutions results in the offender's continued ability to offend, and fails to protect the innocent.

Jail may remain the only alternative for the truly dangerous, but long-winded punishment benefits no one. Although punishment in any form is a crude concept, an offender's freedom should be forfeited, according to the seriousness of the crime. But the enormous costs of confinement would be more usefully spent on supervision of the guilty in making realistic recompense for the victim until the fault is repaid. The perpetrator would be doing something useful and the victim would benefit. If administering such a programme is thought to be impossible, then physical punishment, including short sharp pain has a justifiable place.

And that must include everyone, whatever his place in the pecking order.

Cry for Democracy

Europe and the USA talk a lot about democracy. It may still be the best of inadequate choices, but it's usefulness in providing contented lives is becoming less obvious. The range and complexity of political issues are overwhelming, as are the countless personal wishes of the electorate. Much of the information we obtain stems from the mass-media which is inevitably biased or distorted to suit the agenda of these outlets. The short-term, adversarial political system reduces rational discussion to 'point-scoring', leaving the voter with little understanding of what is important and what is irrelevant or misleading.

The really important matters are decided behind closed doors and are often contrary to public wishes. The voter is effectively disenfranchised, and if he bothers to vote, it will favour what he guesses will be to his immediate advantage, with little consideration given to the longer term effects of his decision.

Misuse of the system has brought disrepute. We were given false information about Iraq and instigated a pre-emptive war. We mourn our own 400 but ignore the 100,000 others who suffered. National security is still dependent on the nuclear deterrent, which risks elimination of humanity.

Cause and effect of climate change remain unclear, and energy policy remains chaotic. We still abuse unrenewable recourses. We still neglect the prospects of rural Britain and encourage further development of overcrowded urban areas.

We do nothing to reduce overall population, and cow-tow to Europe's every wish, including their insistence that limitless immigration must be accepted.

Economic growth has become the God of human aspirations.
It is tragic that establishment has not recognised the damage which massive consumption is causing, all in the misnomer of prosperity. Through ignorance and apathy, tolerable British life is fast deteriorating. Unfortunately there are too many of us. The holy grail of benign dictatorship is unrealistic, so solutions remain with democracy. But our political representatives have become so isolated, so elitist and so subservient to financial and commercial institutions, we are reduced to bit-parts in a remote machine with little influence on policy.

It is the overriding conflict between growth and scarcity which endangers democracy and global diplomacy. Transfer of power from local to central authority, from elected representatives to un-elected lobbyists, from nation governments to international institutions, each with their own axes to grind and each with their powerful self-interests, have reduced democracy to an ineffective mockery. Endemic corruption seals the lid. Government for the people, by the people lacks common integrity and has killed the promising intent.

Democracy requires trust between politician and voter. That requires honesty and public understanding of the issues which are currently causing so much global anguish.

With open minds, the huge facilities of the mass-media could very quickly bring awareness of our true predicament. An honest updated political brief, and a fair voting system could return a measure of trust from the electorate.

It only needs the will to make it happen.

Europe, your Options

The original concept of a European Community, made up of independent nations, cooperating in mutual interests was a feasible possibility. It was influenced by the need to prevent Germany from repeating it's dash for domination for a third time. Coincidental with many other postwar developments, it has prevented war in most of Europe.

It may have been logical to reinforce this new-found stability by closer integration of the half dozen countries involved at that time. They were all recognisably similar in culture and status. Adding more, and yet more countries to the club was thought to be good for potential commercial growth, but it has caused unexpected stresses.

Differences in historic, background, religious views and economic status had evolved over millennia to form legitimate entities. Any understanding of the trauma in sacrificing a country's identity to comply with foreign criteria was absent. Differences can not be homogenised so easily.

Economic union for the original members may still be a valid concept. New additions have been tempted by hand-outs, or at least by the hope of improvement to their economic situations. They were unprepared for such widespread imposition of rules by distant, unelected bureaucrats. Their chances of assimilating with relatively sophisticated countries was never realistic.

Although Britain is influenced by the Union, it retains the possibility of regaining much of it's previous independence. It is the loss of independence and self-determination which has doomed this premature and disaffected set-up of total integration.

The original concept was a pragmatic solution arranged by the victors. In the more settled post-war times, Germany deserves admiration for it's remarkable success in overcoming it's own devastation. However, although it is reputed to be reluctant to take-on leadership, it is now recognised as the principal force in European economic growth, and is continuing to promote the necessity of economic integration.

Whether they like it or not, they have for a third time placed themselves in a dominant position and are trying to force their own aspirations onto others. The crushing and disruptive effects of being told what to do and how to do it by unrelated power, are contrary to peaceful stability. If there is any doubt about the long term effects of foreign authority, in any form, consider the machinations in the Middle East, or even in Ireland's recent history. Imposed solutions, with or without the connivance of local politicians, always causes injustice and resentment which can last for generations.

Continual growth in search of prosperity on a finite world is, in any case, a contradiction in terms. Limits to space, and recourses are real, and will eventually curtail mankind's megalomania.

Get me out of here,

I'm a Proselyte man

Europe's integration has no empathy with humanity. It is just one more undemocratic conglomerate, bent on material wealth, from which only the powerful gain.

It does, however, contain all the varied elements for more optimistic ways of living. Our differences are not trivial. They deserve respect, co-operation and enhancement, rather than enforcement into bland uniformity.

Genuine democratic co-operation would provide a sane reason for it's existence.

Climate change Claptrap

Study of tree rings and core ice samples from the polar regions prove that climate has varied over the centuries. Reasons include variations in solar radiation, earthly volcanic activity and meteor impacts. Movement in the earths molten core, wobble about it's axis and forest fires have also contributed.

Recent man-made carbon greenhouse effect is thought to have artificially increased warming., but it's relative effect in the context of other fundamental natural influences remains in doubt. Whether clean fuels make any appreciable difference to naturally occurring changes is not in the long run of much consequence.

Other man-made changes are likely to have more immediate and equally damaging effects on the good health of civilisation and on the earth itself, and cosmic changes remain an on-going threat. Present dash for clean energy can not solve the huge and growing demand for material consumption. In any case, reduction of carbon emissions is not possible without global acquiescence, and that will remain beyond the wit of man until the global predicament of overpopulation is understood.

The west and developing nations are set to increase use of fossil fuels, which although diminishing, remain abundant. They overwhelm any minor advantage that clean fuels provide. Energy requirement is so huge that solar, hydro and wind sources can not meet requirements. The only available alternative fuel is nuclear, which is potentially devastating due to it's radioactivity.

Successful development and use of fuel, from whichever source, clean or dirty, on such a large scale will only continue to encourage yet more growth. It is this growth, with it's insatiable demands on material sustenance and consequent destruction of natural earthly systems which needs global attention.

Thinking to reduce climate change is no more sane than asking the tides to stop.

If we expect to survive the human plague, it is overall population and massive consumption which has to be reduced. Without that, our attempts to obtain the good life are a waste of intellect, education and effort. Those who rule seem unable to see that they, and the rest of us who provide their wealth, are inter-dependant and that we all depend on cohesion of society and the good health of our planet.

No effort has yet been made to ameliorate the probability of rising sea levels, and tsunamis, nor of volcanic activity and extreme weather. No one has found a safe solution to the use of nuclear power, nor for the storage of nuclear waste. No one has made any serious attempt to reduce the mountains of waste discarded by affluent humanity and in the mean time the biodiversity of flora and fauna is being destroyed at an ever increasing rate.

There is little we can do to avoid meteor impact, but building on flood-plains, in coastal regions and on river banks has become an invitation for disaster due to the huge numbers now occupying these areas. Likewise, settlements in earthquake regions and close to volcanoes have grown so much that disasters are inevitable. Even the security of safe lands has become vulnerable to extreme weather due to the large number of residents now occupying these areas.

We are looking through the wrong end of the telescope. Understanding and acceptance of the forces of nature would, in the long-run, benefit us far more than pretending those forces can be manipulated to suit our condition. It is time to acknowledge our impotence in challenging the power of nature, and to put a stop to the spiralling momentum of growth so that compatibility with our world may be achieved.

Energetic waste of Energy

The universe and life it contains is now known to consist entirely of energy. Of all it's many forms, life is the only element where consciousness is present, and only human life which has been able to exploit it. Our own earth contains many forms of energy which are influenced by our sun as well as the wider cosmos. The entire melee is inter-dependent, as are we on our own small planet.

Since discovery of fire, evolving communities have found and used ever more sources of energy, which have allowed progress to larger and more sophisticated civilisations. But success has had the unforeseen consequence of rapidly increasing population, with it's insatiable appetites. Finding new sources of energy is no longer humanity's most urgent problem, neither is climate change, whatever is causing it. The mistaken assumption that limitless growth can be accommodated on our limited planet is now the paramount problem. This has become the stumbling block to all our potential aspirations.

We are primarily dependent on the physical bounty of the natural planet, and on mankind's ability to co-operate. The time for survival of the fittest is over. We are approaching full capacity which the momentum of growth will over-run if not controlled.

Like children playing with grown-up toys, the amazing products of science and technology are used carelessly to exploit treasures on which we will always depend. They assist our chores and amuse our spare time, but the transient pleasures of novelty are soon forgotten, to be replaced with yet more powerful throw-aways while trash and boredom proliferate.

Since the 'Big Bang', our universe has been reverting to a state of uniform simplicity, ie, from dust back to dust. What went before is gone for ever. Options for the future are consequently reduced and become progressively vulnerable to natural calamities and human mistakes. Individual species do not normally notice environmental change as the earth slowly ages. But through indiscriminate use of energy we have caused rapid changes which now endanger all life.

Unprecedented rapid growth continues to destroy the planet while fundamental, simple aspirations of humanity are ignored.

Stop-gap solutions to energy shortage or to reduce carbon emissions give a false sense of security. Energy is everywhere, just waiting to be discovered. It is the care-less way we use it that needs attention. The underlying problem of massive consumption is where our energies need to be directed.

Physical skills are being wasted on the pushing of electric buttons to control a plethora of automated gadgets which burn toxic fuel, and cause us to become lazy and fat in the process. Our neglected physical abilities are highly developed and require expression.

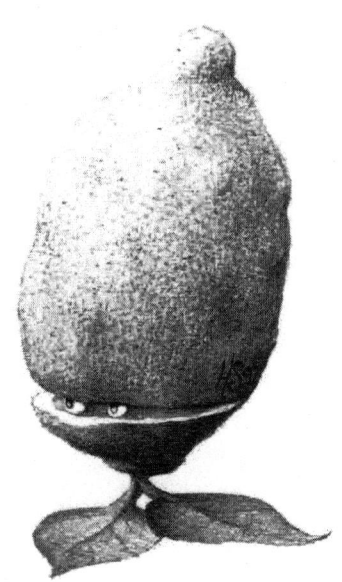

Human energy could be far more usefully engaged in productive, rewarding work, rather than allowing automation to render us redundant. It is ourselves who need to be intelligent, not our robots.

If we are here only to achieve maximum self-gratification, and in the process to prematurely destroy ourselves, then bring-on Armageddon and let's get it over with.

Otherwise, take a closer look at where our exploits are leading. We may be clever but it wisdom that is needed to overcome the dilemmas we face.

Wages of Sin

Reward for one by helping another has existed since life began. Development would not have been possible without mutual, if unconscious, co-operation between as well as within species.

Remuneration for labour, skill, effort and responsibility is an extension of the process. It enabled progress in a sustainable manner according to abilities and available sustenance.

But reward for assistance requires mutual agreement on the value of the service. If unfairly or thoughtlessly balanced, it results in disadvantage for someone and invites deprivation and dispute.

Increasing prosperity has encouraged expectation of continued improvement. It is now normal to receive regular increases, just for attending your post. Why ? when the amount of work effort has not changed. It is made worse as these increases are on a percentage basis which advantages those who are all ready better-off. Discrepancy, greed and corruption are built into the system.

Progress has depended on innovation and exploitation, not on improved intelligence, effort or responsibility. Potential abilities and basic requirements of mankind are the same now as for primeval man. It is the environment which changes as innovation proceeds.

The usefulness of an individual relates to his benefit to mankind, and his abilities deserve to be recognised. But he remains a man, not a God. His reward should never give him unwarranted power over his contemporaries as this is not only contentious, it usurps democracy.

Current methods of remuneration amount to blatant egoism. It is made worse by borrowing to maintain 'present progress'. Borrowing implicitly risks reneging which makes the individual, the tax-payer or the next generation obliged to pay-off the debt. To pretend that spurious economic manipulation can substitute the true value of materials and services is insane abuse of power. And that is why our present economy is in debt, amounting to £trillions.

In relation to the true value of limited habitable-pace, clean water, finite raw materials and the planet's good health, we have valued ourselves in a grossly selfish, short-term and inflated manner. Through capitalism, our system of remuneration has successfully produced a 'something for nothing' culture where universal requirement to balance the books has been replaced by the facility of credit. Indiscriminate exploitation of men and materials, and unfair distribution of the benefits has caused a nightmare of unsustainable conditions for this and future generations.

Economic systems are all presently dependent on continuation of the momentum of growth. They are only succeeding to maintain present growth by extortionate borrowing from an imaginary 'bank of mirrors.' It is a process which has all ready built-up debt and earthly destruction that can not be replenished in monetary terms.

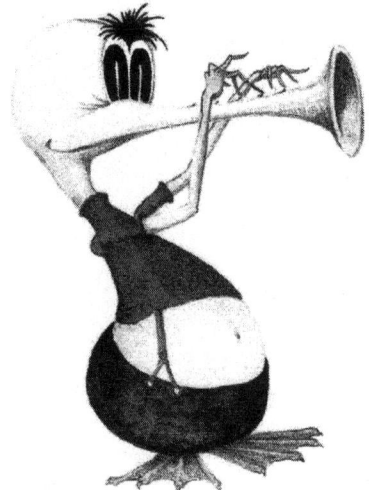

Optimism to continue the process is inane folly, because the implacable requirement of nature to balance it's books will eventually, like Shylock, extract it's pound of flesh in literal terms.

This madness can only be saved by radical global agreement to rebalance values and methods of remuneration compatible with our finite, physical realities.

Population, problem or Paranoia

How can it be that persistent, compounding growth is perceived to be the only acceptable route to prosperity ?   It's past successes have only advantaged about half the population and caused universal strife, widespread deprivation and irreversible damage to natural earthly elements. Huge consumption is killing the goose which is still expected to continue laying the golden eggs.

In 'round figures', world population reached the first Billion in 1850, after 40,000 years of human development. In 1960, only 100 or so years later, there were 3 Billion. Since then, population has exploded, rising in only 50 years to 7 Billion. Our generation is experiencing the greatest change to life on earth since the dinosaurs' demise. Why is this devastating issue being ignored ?

Procreation is the purpose of life. But all our aspirations now depend on conscious continuation of growth, without being willing to accept that corresponding timely death is a necessary counter-balancing requirement. The young who have only known conditions of rapid change may regard this as normal. But normal it is not. The old have seen their world change beyond recognition. Where there used to be space, opportunity and time to adjust, there is now no time to adjust and attempts to accommodate overcrowding, stressed services and shortages of basic needs are increasing the probability of strife and war.

In recent decades many have enjoyed healthier and longer life, but growing disparity between rich and poor is dividing communities and leaving the masses to suffer the consequences of scarcity, conflict and devastation. The pattern is repeated world-wide. Optimists hope that all will be lifted out of poverty when prosperity and women's education will negate need of large families.   They anticipate population will reach 9 to 11 Billion and then begin to reduce.

In the mean time, those Billions will still require the means to survive. The momentum of growth will not suddenly be resolved by overnight adaptation to sustainability. Our evident inability to co-operate in an altruistic sharing of recourses is far more likely to increase divisions, conflict and pitiless self-interest.

To prevent chaos in the future, adapting to sustainable solutions has to be considered now. Reliance on primitive instinct has resulted in a human plague, and plagues are not sustainable. Humanity has to come to understand the impossibility of perpetual growth within the confines of our planet's limited capacity.

The most basic function of reproduction is not in question, but control over numbers produced has become essential. Birth control and abortion have become universally necessary. Squeamish refusal to talk about euthanasia and allowing death to take it's natural course is prolonging the build-up of excessive numbers. The niceties of human rights have ignored the wishes of those who want to die, and the living nightmare of billions who starve in diseased squalor.

To ignore the probability of civil collapse amounts to wishful thinking, reminiscent of Nero's playing while Rome burned, but it is much worse as now, there is nowhere else to go.

You may think this outlook is too pessimistic as science in the past has always found a way of catching up with events. But this is very different. There has never been a conflict involving such large numbers searching for diminishing space and recourses. We need a miracle. Honest discussion about this deadly subject could yet produce one.

Art or Artful

There was once good reason to scratch marks on cave walls, to chisel and mould, and to draw and paint. Early expressions of art were regarded as powerful magic, which elevated the artisan to god like status. They became secure in the upper echelons of dynasties and revered in the company of kings.

Of the many creative outlets, the visual arts have always received exceptional attention, based initially on it's usefulness to those in power. But since the advent of printing and photography, it's usefulness as a means to promote the powerful has diminished. Yet it remains revered. After a lifetime of trying to understand, I remain confused by the roll of art today.

It appears that art has become an end in itself, isolated from it's former usefulness but admired for it's exaggerated value. It now excludes any aspect of practically useful design and includes items of absolute folly. It has been taken out of it's natural historic context to be placed in serried ranks for voyeurism or locked in basements to accumulate wealth.

This disingenuous view has to be modified. The urge to create has moved on to science and technology, leaving the artist with nowhere to go. But even if art has no definable purpose, some of it is worthy of our admiration.

Art, to be worthy of the title, implies a subject made with recognisable skill and to have some relevance to life or aspirations. So much of what I see lacks talent, knowledge and effort, and the more extreme examples have no place in this field. They say that beauty is in the eye of the beholder, but does art need to be beautiful? Well, yes it does. The forms, proportions, compositions and colours of the natural world are embedded in the human psyche.

All our successful endeavours have been influenced, and indeed are subconsciously controlled, by the forces which nature imposes. To deliberately, or accidentally deviate from these constraints, results in meaningless chaos which is foreign to our appreciation and wellbeing. Damien's shark, would be better placed in separate halls, such as Madam Tussaud's. There will always be space for the whimsical, but to elevate it to the status of genius is just silly.

Promotion of art is now driven by the entrepreneur who has a vested interest in escalating it's value. There is a 'Kings clothes syndrome' active in today's market which distorts the value of real talent and subordinates the artist in favour of marketing forces.

The essence of creativity is in it's usefulness to mankind, the essence of art is in it's ability to enlighten our day. The artificial value of art, as promoted by the entrepreneur, has become a self perpetuating nonsense. It is admired because we are told it is worthy, and purchased because of it's contrived value, irrespective of it's true merit. There is a lack of genuine appreciation of the work itself.

Much of true art has 'trade' association which now seems to eliminate it from public viewing. Magnificent works of art, having practical relevance to life, have been produced since the pre-Christian civilisations and continued to flourish throughout the industrial revolution to the present techno-explosion. Where are they ?

While we are presented with daub, appearing to lack the benefit of good eye sight, masterpieces are shut away in filing cabinets.

Sadly, the Turner Prize has become the symbol of mankind's stupidity.

Reach for the stars, or Starve

Since Dan Dare and the Mekon enthralled childhood, and since Sputnik converted wishful thinking to reality, developments in space have become part of daily life on which we now depend. Since primordial slime developed into higher life forms, the force to grow, innovate and explore has been irresistible. Life can not stand still. It is compelled to grow until it's allotted time or it's sustenance is exhausted.

Empirical luck has determined whether any individual species develops or dies. Over the ages, successful behaviour became instinctive, but those instincts can become too entrenched to adapt to sudden changes.

Our species retains ancient instincts which still control most of our behaviour. But our instinct to act or react in deeply entrenched ways is influenced by conscious thought. We possess self-determination and imagination to make independent choices. This has allowed development of complex civilisations. But, 'Nassa, we have a problem'. It has also allowed thoughtless expansion. We have enthusiastically embraced progress without recognising the trap that primitive instinct has laid.

As with all life, we produce more seed than can possibly develop, but instinct forces us to maximise our chances. As knowledge and numbers increase, habitat and sustenance is relentlessly reduced. The surplus seeds will fail, either through lack of sustenance or by our realisation that deliberate controls have become necessary. The parameters of all life do have limits.

Although intelligence-driven innovation has attempted to keep pace with demands, the battle is being lost. Human activity has for the first time, artificially endangered prospects for future healthy existence.

It has now been seriously suggested that space exploration is developed to find new sources of raw material, and in the longer term, to find other planets that may be suitable for human habitation.

Although exploration is inevitable and desirable, the concept of saving the world by exploitation of other planets is so costly and so far in the future that it is irrelevant to our present impoverished situation.

Here on earth, little thought is given to ordinary humanitarian necessities. While the fortunate enjoy life at the leading edge of scientific and social development, the majority are submerged in a bland miasma of mediocrity, deprivation and appalling waste. If continuation of life depends on an elite minority leading the rest of us to the promised land, what happens to the billions who can not make it ?   We are carelessly engineering our own premature demise.

Would it not be better to acknowledge the inter-dependent nature of life on earth, and to use our rare gift of intelligence more altruistically ? Our abilities are presently being stifled by out-dated instincts while intelligence is being wasted on self-aggrandizement.

Since the 60's, as new freedoms spread, attitudes of mind have become careless and greedy. A simplistic assumption that humanity had conquered nature and that prosperity for all was just around the corner has lead to our present invidious situation.

Humanity's need   to feel and express our finer, emotional characteristics have been swamped by the pressures of daily life. Science may still provide our material needs, but the soul requires sensitive, disciplined thought and action on where and how to use it. Before thinking to inflicting our abuses on other unsuspecting
planets, we have to come to terms with our own man-made predicaments, here on our own fragile earth.

Our Civil Scenarios

No matter when we live, we think we have lived in the best of times. Throughout history, except for the intrusion of war and disease, standards of health and living conditions have gradually improved as innovations developed.

Agriculture, medicine, hygiene, technology and communications have allowed progress to sophisticated society. New sources of energy have provided the raw power to accelerate development. Military innovations, intended for destruction, have also enhanced material advancement in civilised life. Nowadays, lack of pain, cures for almost everything and abundance of material facilities have allowed populations to prosper. There are many who do not benefit, but the momentum of growth is expected to provide prosperity for all in due course.

At the time of the industrial revolution, this outlook may have been valid. Up to the 1960's it may still have had merit. Since then, success has allowed population to increase so rapidly, in such a short time, that provision of basic requirements are deteriorating. For the first time there are global shortages of habitable space, clean water, and material sustenance.

Growth has not been in a regular upward straight line which would have given time to plan and adjust to changing circumstances. It is a compounding growth which forms a quickly rising curve where time to adjust is reduced as consumption expands. It is not mathematically possible to continue the momentum when the upward curve approaches vertical. Something has to give-way.

We have become dependent on a momentum of growth which is not sustainable. Unless there is unprecedented reversal of the trend, hopes of a better life will be swamped by sheer weight of numbers and by the planet's unavoidable deterioration.

Some say that global population has begun to reduce, but the huge number of children all ready living will increase numbers for the next 25 to 50 years. Considering present stresses, a further increase of 20% in such a short time indicates that we will be the first to live in deteriorating times.

There appear to be three possible future scenarios.
1. Present growth trends continue, eventually causing collapse of civil social systems through excessive exploitation, conflict and destruction of the natural biosphere.
2. Individual nations or groups gain overall power and close ranks to protect and control their own economies. Sustainability is achieved by exploiting the rest of humanity, or abandoning it to it's fate.
3. We come to our senses in an altruistic renaissance. This could only be achieved, first by understanding the predicament we are in, then by unprecedented co-operation in reducing population and consumption to levels that could be realistically maintained.

We are in a fix, and there is no easy option. Personal freedoms, science and technology have inadvertently resulted in un-sustainable growth.

Adaptation to 'growth reduction' is the greatest challenge which any living matter could face.

We at least have the intelligence to try it. At present, our entrenched primitive instincts prevent it from happening.

'The power and the glory
of all matter
consists in obedience,
not in freedom...
The sun has no liberty,
a dead leaf has much'.

Although brief and simplistic, this booklet
reveals the essence of mankind's dilemma.
If you think I am mistaken,... tell me why.
If you agree,...do something about it.

Where have the Ethics of Growth been lost

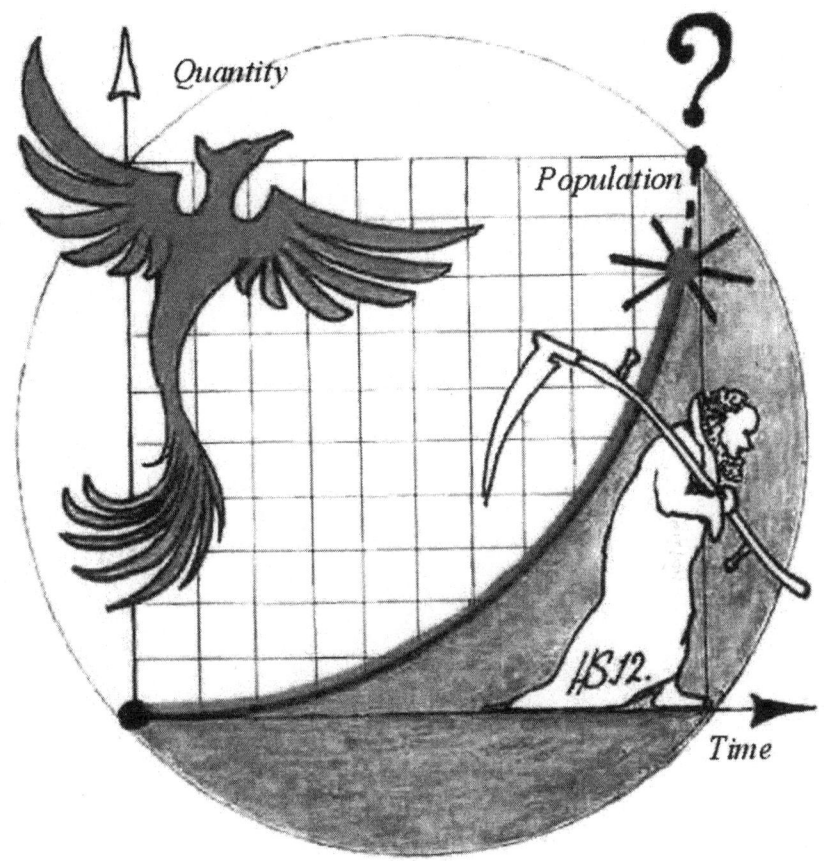

Motif, indicating the vulnerable place where 7 billion inhabitants exist on the exponential graph.

Now that you have read it, read it again,... slowly.

Edwards Brothers Malloy
Oxnard, CA USA
September 8, 2015